TALES FROM THE TUNDRA

A COLLECTION OF INUIT STORIES

RETOLD BY **IBI KASLIK**

ILLUSTRATED BY **ANTHONY BRENNAN**

FOREWORD BY **LOUISE FLAHERTY**

INHABIT
MEDIA

PUBLISHED BY INHABIT MEDIA INC.
www.inhabitmedia.com

Editors: Louise Flaherty and Neil Christopher

Design/Art Direction: Danny Christopher

Inhabit Media Inc. (Iqaluit), P.O. Box 11125, Iqaluit, Nunavut, X0A 1H0
(Toronto), 146A Orchard View Blvd., Toronto, Ontario, M4R 1C3

Printed and Bound in Canada

Library and Archives Canada Cataloguing in Publication

Kaslik, Ibolya, 1973-
Tales from the tundra : a collection of Inuit stories / retold by
Ibi Kaslik ; illustrated by Anthony Brennan ; foreword by Louise
Flaherty.

ISBN 978-1-926569-15-4

1. Inuit--Folklore. 2. Legends--Arctic regions.
I. Brennan, Anthony, 1978- II. Title.

E99.E7K366 2010   j398.2089'9712   C2010-905946-8

CONTENTS

REGIONS OF NUNAVUT

1 KITIKMEOT
2 KIVALLIQ
3 QIKIQTANI

FOREWORD

The stories retold in this book are part of a very old, very rich mythology passed down by Inuit elders.

Storytellers from all cultures are very imaginative folk, and Inuit storytellers are no exception. A good storyteller will tell stories that bring their audience's imagination to life, and this is what Inuit elders did with their tales.

At bedtime, grandparents would share with children the stories that they had heard from their elders, and their elders before them. During blizzards, a storyteller might start a story and children would gather around on their sleeping platform and listen with interest to riveting tales of mythical beings, or epic journeys.

Through our myths and legends, children learned the dangers of straying too far from their parents, discovered how various animals were created, and were told the origins of the moon, sun, stars, and Inuit constellations. Inuit myths and legends are very important to Inuit. They are part of our culture and our history. This book offers kids and parents alike the chance to experience a little bit of that tradition.

The contemporary retellings of traditional tales in this book will make these stories available to younger folk who may not have the chance to hear many of the stories from their families. As you read through this book, remember that each region of the Arctic has its own unique version of each story.

I hope you enjoy these stories, and that you pass them along to others as they have been passed to you.

Louise Flaherty
Publisher, Inhabit Media Inc.

This story explains how a smart and crafty siksik—a ground squirrel found in the arctic—was able to trick a very hungry owl. This version of the story comes from the Qikiqtani region of Nunavut.

THE OWL AND
THE SIKSIK

Once there was an owl that hunted siksiks, as many owls do. Unfortunately for the owl and his family, it had been a long time since he had caught a siksik. Today, the owl decided, would be different. He would catch a siksik! How proud and well fed his family would be!

"Siksiks often go in and out of their dens," thought the owl, believing himself to be very clever. "Today I will find a siksik den and wait there until I see one."

The owl found a siksik den and waited next to the opening, patiently. Finally, when the little squirrel darted out of its hole, the owl blocked the entrance of the den so that the siksik could not go back in. The siksik stood still, paralyzed with fear.

The owl planted one foot on each side of the doorway and shouted confidently to his owl family: "Bring two sleds! I have trapped a siksik! Come! Let us load the qamutiit with our catch!"

"You are so excited and so happy," said the siksik, who had recovered from his fear. "Why don't you do a dance?"

"Yes, siksik! I am so happy. I will finally have some meat! Yes, you are right. I should dance!"

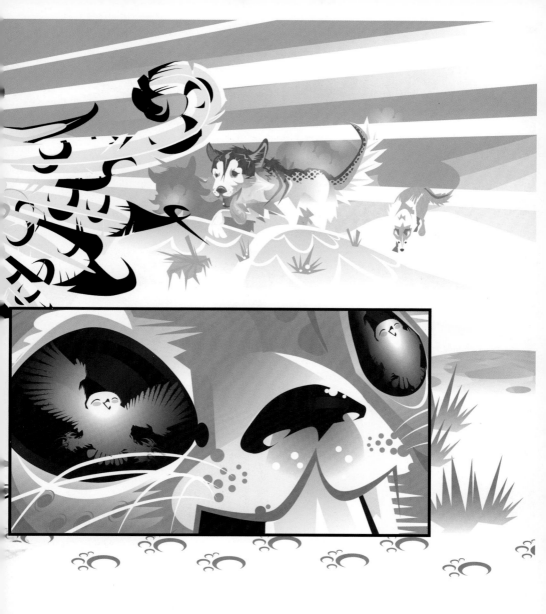

Hopping from one foot to another, the owl danced a grateful dance.

"Ah, yes, look at the sky and dance," laughed the siksik. "But spread your legs, owl. Make more room and dance faster to show your joy!"

The owl did as the siksik told him. He danced even faster.

The siksik again sang out to the owl, who was lost in his joyful prancing, "Look at the sky and dance, owl! Spread your legs. Make more room and dance faster."

The owl jumped and danced his happy dance, thinking only of the delicious feast that awaited him after he killed this silly siksik. He spread his legs further apart as he bopped and hopped from foot to foot. But he forgot to watch the daring siksik.

Seeing his chance at last, the siksiit dashed through the owl's legs. He hurried into his den without a backward look.

When he was safely inside his den, the siksik chirped happily, as siksiks are known to do. When the owl heard the siksik's little chirp, the owl realized he had been tricked. Disappointed, he yelled, "Dog teams go back, go back! Our dinner has escaped."

In this story, an old woman creates caribou and walrus so that her people will have more animals to hunt. This version of the story comes from the Qikiqtani region of Nunavut

HOW THE CARIBOU AND
THE WALRUS CAME TO BE

This story took place somewhere in the Arctic, many, many years ago.

Once, an old woman sat in her iglu and thought, "Our people need more animals to hunt. We need more animals to feed our families and more hides to keep us warm during the cold, long winter."

She pondered this challenge until an idea struck her: "I know!" she thought, "I will transform my old sealskin jacket into a walrus!" The old woman did exactly that: she made a walrus from her own coat. But when she looked at it closely, she thought it didn't look exactly right so she put antlers on its head and placed it in the water. It looked fine now, she decided. She was satisfied with the creature she had created.

Then the old woman said to herself, "I will transform my trousers into a caribou!" Again, she did just as she had said: she made a caribou from her pants. The dark part of her trousers became the animal's back, while the white part served as its belly. With the waistband, she made legs. Once again, she examined the newly made animal and decided it did not please her exactly. So, she put tusks in its mouth and sent it free to roam everywhere. It looked fine now, she decided, satisfied with the creature she had created.

One day, the caribou saw a hunter approaching. The caribou was unafraid of the man and it ran up to him and speared the hunter with its pointed tusks. The injured hunter ran home and told the community what had occurred.

When the hunter told the old woman about his frightening encounter with the caribou, she became very angry.

The old woman called the walrus and the caribou and they came to her. She took the antlers off the walrus and placed them on the caribou's head. She then pulled the tusks from the caribou's mouth and pushed them into the walrus's mouth.

She admired her work before she removed a few of the caribou's teeth and kicked its forehead flat until its eyes protruded, as punishment for having hurt the hunter. Then she told the caribou, "You will never come near the walrus. You will stay inland, far away from the water. And, whenever you smell the scent of a hunter, you will be afraid!"

This is how the walrus and caribou came to inhabit our land and the reason why, whenever a caribou smells a man, it is afraid.

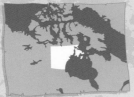

In Nunavut, people from different regions have different stories about how animals were created. In this story, which comes from the Kivalliq region of Nunavut, the first caribou come from a hole in the ground created by an earth spirit looking for food for his wife.

ORIGIN OF THE CARIBOU

In the early days, there were no large animals on the tundra. Our ancestors could only hunt small animals: foxes, lemmings, siksiks, and rabbits.

Many years ago, a stranger came to a small Inuit village. He appeared kind and so was asked to stay by the villagers. After awhile, he married a local woman. At first, all was well with the couple until the woman realized that the stranger did not hunt. The stranger's wife grew hungry, cold, and tired. She had no food to eat, no skins to make warm clothing, and no oil for her qulliq. Soon, the villagers became tired and frustrated because they had to take care of the stranger's wife.

Still, the villagers understood that the stranger was not simply lazy. They knew the stranger was not a man at all but an earth spirit, which was why he did not have any use for hunting. The earth spirit could eat rocks and sand in order to survive.

One day, the elders of the village explained to the stranger that it was his responsibility to hunt animals for his wife. So, early the next morning, the stranger headed out onto the land to hunt.

Not long after, the stranger returned to the village. He carried a large, unusual animal on his back. The people of the village did not know what to make of this new animal. It had hooves and had sharp antlers on its head. It was a caribou, but no one had ever seen one before, so they did not even know what to call it. They soon discovered that it had delicious meat on its bones and that the caribou's fur could be used to make warm clothing. The stranger's wife was very happy, indeed, with her husband.

The other hunters in the village wondered how this lazy hunter had caught such a useful and magnificent animal. Where had he found it? Were there more?

After a few days, the stranger's wife asked him to bring home another caribou, so he headed out to hunt but, this time, the hunter did not go alone. He was followed by one of the village hunters. The jealous hunter was determined to find out where the caribou lived and how these animals could be hunted.

When the stranger was out of sight of the village, he took out his knife and stuck it into the earth while the other hunter wondered why the stranger did this.

Suddenly, a caribou jumped out of the hole! The stranger quickly killed the animal and covered the hole. He then put the caribou on his shoulder and walked back toward the village.

As soon as the stranger was out of sight, the other hunter crept over to the spot where the hole had been. Nervous, he took out his knife and dragged it along the ground, just as the stranger had. Without warning, a caribou leaped out of the hole, as if by magic! The hunter rose to his feet and grabbed the animal. He had caught one! However, in his excitement, he had forgotten to cover the hole.

Within seconds, many caribou began to jump out of the hole. At first, caribou were jumping up one or two at a time, but after a few minutes, a steady stream of caribou were climbing out of the hole, rising up through in an unstoppable flow of hooves, fur, and antlers. Finally free, the caribou began to run wildly across the land.

The hunter dropped his knife and sprinted toward the village.

Meanwhile, the stranger's wife and her family were admiring the second magnificent caribou he had caught, but they were interrupted by the jealous hunter's screams in the distance. "Stranger, the caribou have escaped!"

Thousands of caribou galloped across the hills. The hunter dropped the caribou and walked inland, toward the herd. He felt angry yet responsible as he was worried that one day these fierce new animals, with their large, pointed antlers, would hurt the people. When he got close to the excited beasts, he drew upon all his magic as he whispered, "Be timid. Be afraid of humans and run away from them, always!"

The raging wind carried the stranger's words to the ears of all the new beautiful animals that had escaped from the magical gash. Suddenly, they lost their confidence and became timid. Almost at once, they began to move inland, away from the human hunters. Though the stranger's wife spent many days searching for her husband, she never found him. No one ever saw the stranger again.

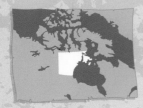

This story explains why ravens and loons
look the way they do today. This version
of the story comes from the Kivalliq
region of Nunavut.

THE RAVEN AND THE LOON

One day, Loon came across her old friend Raven.

"Raven," said Loon, "why do you have so many different coloured skins with you?"

"I sew them into beautiful clothing," Raven explained.

"I sew clothes too!" exclaimed Loon, proudly. "Let us make clothes for each other!"

And so, they agreed.

They prepared the thread for sewing. "I see you rub your thread in soot from the qulliq just as I do," noticed Loon.

"Yes," Raven answered.

When Raven's thread was completely covered with soot, she took out her needle and began to stitch Loon's feathers. Raven passed the needle in and out of Loon's feathers with speed and skill. Tikki tikki, tak tak, tikki tikki, tak tak. Tik-tak, tik-tak!

Soon the beautiful seam was wrapped all around Loon's body. This is the reason Loons are speckled!

When Raven was finished, Loon took the needle and said to her friend, "I am slow and careful, Raven. Be sure to remain still."

Loon began her slow work on Raven. Tik.......tik...... tik...... tak......

"Please, sew faster!" impatient Raven pleaded.

"Sit still!" insisted Loon. "I must concentrate on each stitch."

But Raven would not sit still.

"You must not move!" yelled Loon.

Yet Raven continued to thrash about restlessly, flapping her wings and flipping her tail in a fit of flying feathers.

Finally, Loon lost her patience. She picked up the lamp and poured the black oil onto Raven. Raven was covered in black all over.

"Caw! Caw!" Raven cried, "You have covered me in darkness!"

Raven was furious! She picked up a stone and threw it at Loon. The stone struck Loon in the legs. Loon doubled over in pain, her legs were badly wounded. This is why loons have so much trouble walking on land and prefer to remain in the water.

And this is the story of how these animals came to be as they are today.

In this story, a grandmother accidentally scares her grandson into becoming a little bird. This version of how the ptarmigan and the snow bunting came to be comes from the Qikiqtani region of Nunavut.

5

THE PTARMIGAN AND THE SNOW BUNTING

One evening, a young boy asked his grandmother to tell him a bedtime story.

"Go to bed! I have no story to tell you!" the grandmother replied, irritated by her grandson's request.

The boy began to cry. "Please, Grandmother, just one story. Then I will go to sleep. I promise."

"Very well," the grandmother thought to herself, "I will tell him a frightening and strange story so he will never bother me for a story again!" The old woman leaned in closely to her grandson and whispered in his ear, "I will tell you a story about a lemming that had no hair."

"Grandmother, that is so weird! A lemming with no hair?"

The grandmother nodded. "It had no hair because it was very young," she explained. "It used to live right there, on the porch," she said, pointing to a spot on the porch. "The little lemming was very cold because it was hairless. It begged and begged to stay under my arm to keep warm. One night, when it was time for bed, the lemming jumped into my warm armpit, squirmed around and squealed, too-too-too!"

As soon as the grandmother finished her story, she jumped up and tickled her Grandson playfully.

The boy was so surprised that he leaped out of his bed and transformed into a tiny snow bunting! He tried to yell, but he could only chirp like a bird. Terrified, he flew out of the iglu and disappeared into the freezing cold night.

The old woman rushed outside to search for her grandson. "Where are you, grandson, where?" she asked the empty night. But there was no answer. She could not find him anywhere. Finally, after many hours of fruitless searching, she gave up and returned home.

Tired and cold, the grandmother sat down on the ice and began to cry. Tears ran down her sad wrinkled face and she rubbed her eyes roughly with her old gnarled hands. She cried, on and on into the night, until her eyes became red as fresh blood on white snow.

Because of her sadness and grief, the old woman was transformed into a ptarmigan. The red mark over the ptarmigan's eye is said to originate from the grandmother's red, weeping eyes. The ptarmigan's squawk, "Nauk, aauk!" is said to be an imitation of the grandmother's helpless cry.

And this is how the first snow bunting and ptarmigan came to be.

Ibi Kaslik

Ibi Kaslik is an internationally published novelist and freelance writer. Her recent novel, *The Angel Riots*, was nominated for Ontario's Trillium award (2009). Her first novel, *Skinny*, was a New York Times bestseller. Ibi teaches creative writing at the University of Toronto's School of Continuing Studies.

Anthony Brennan

Anthony Brennan is a Sheridan-trained illustrator who lives in the Toronto area. He has illustrated several books and works as a freelance web designer.